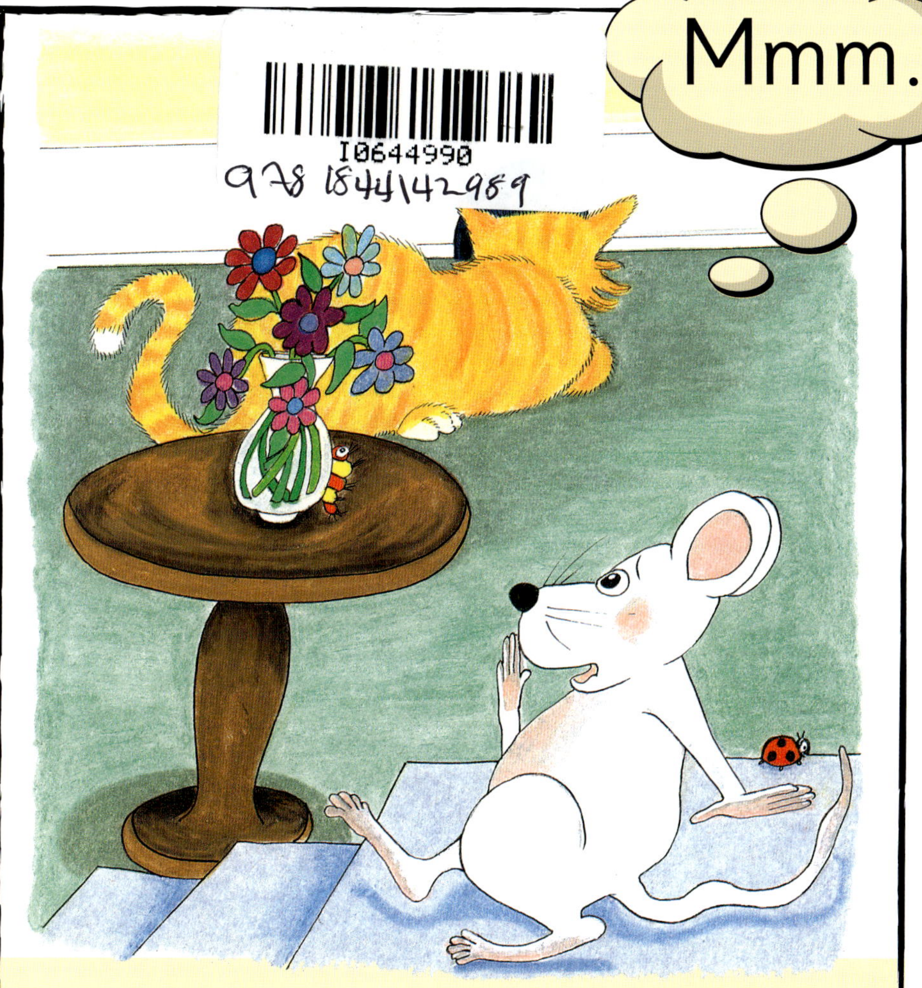

The mouse sees
the cat.

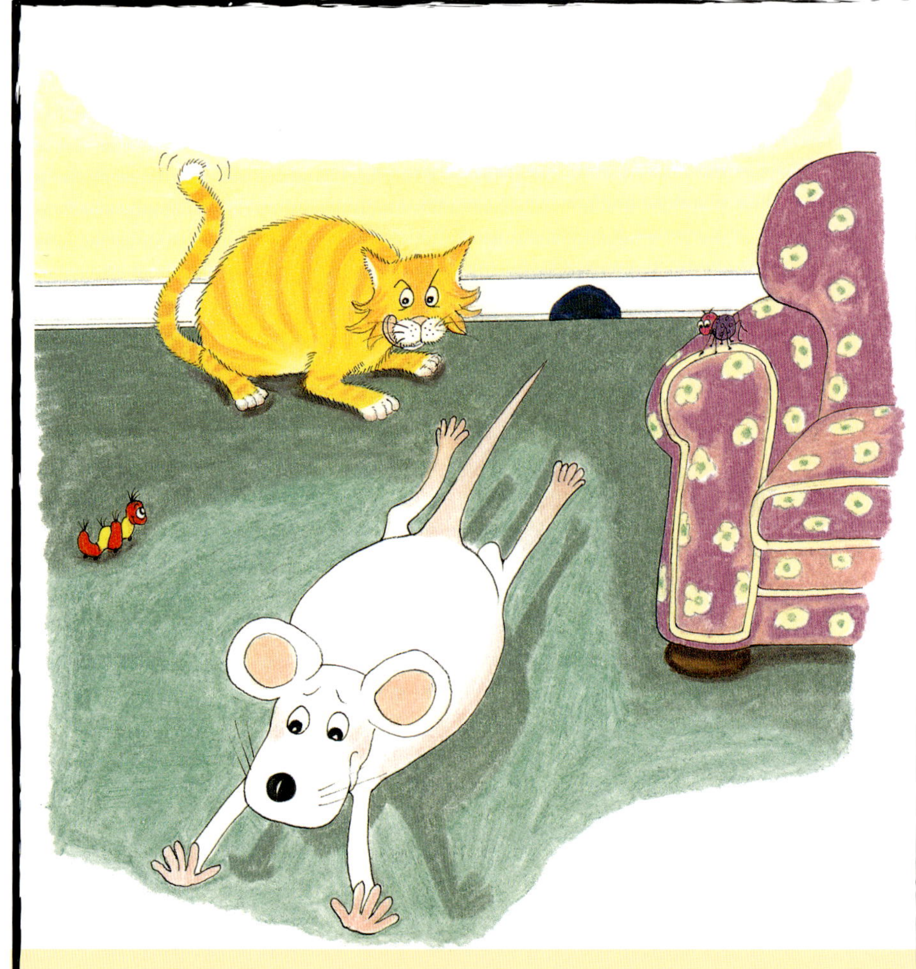

She runs from the cat.

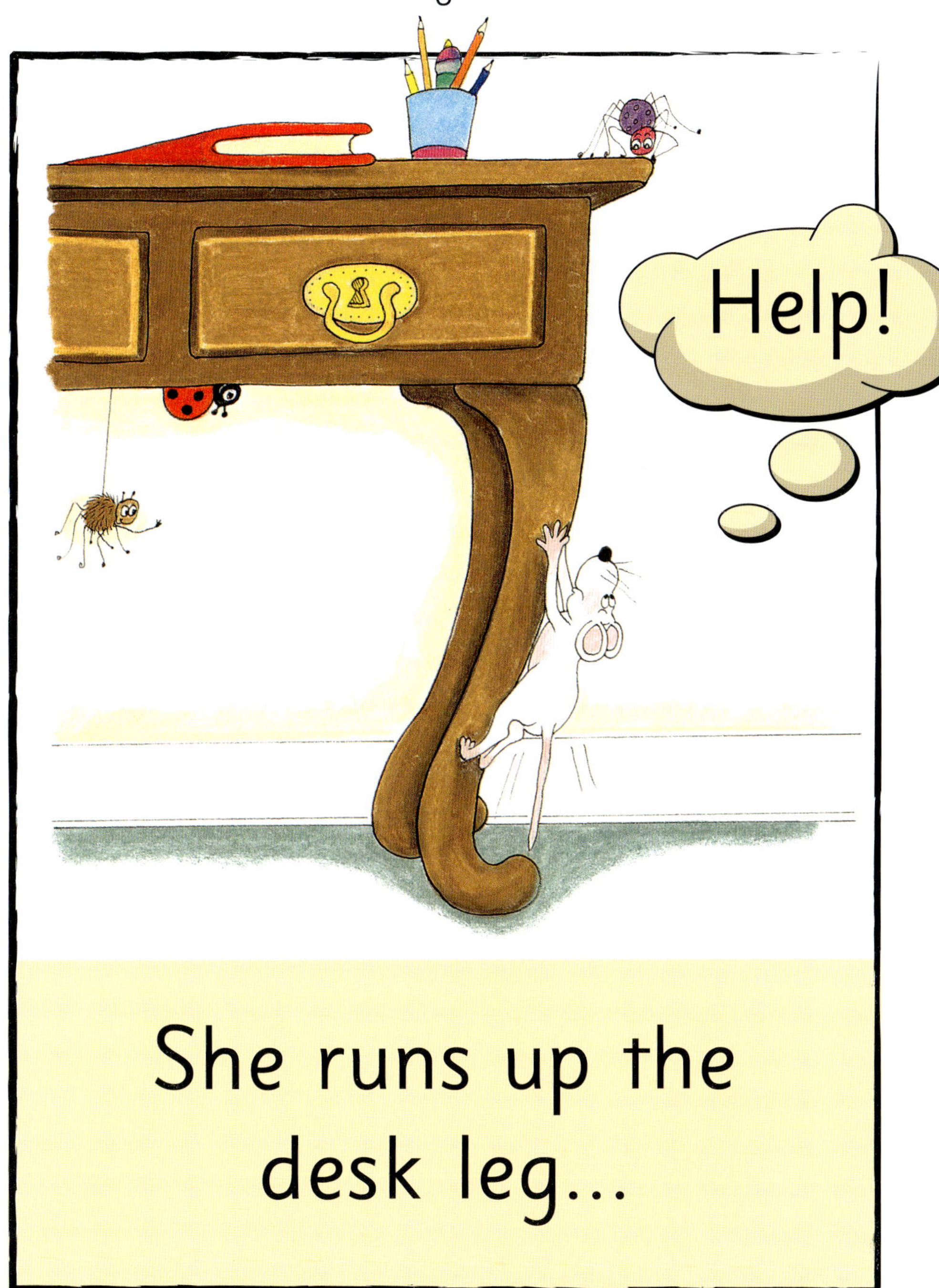

She runs up the desk leg...

...and across the desk top.

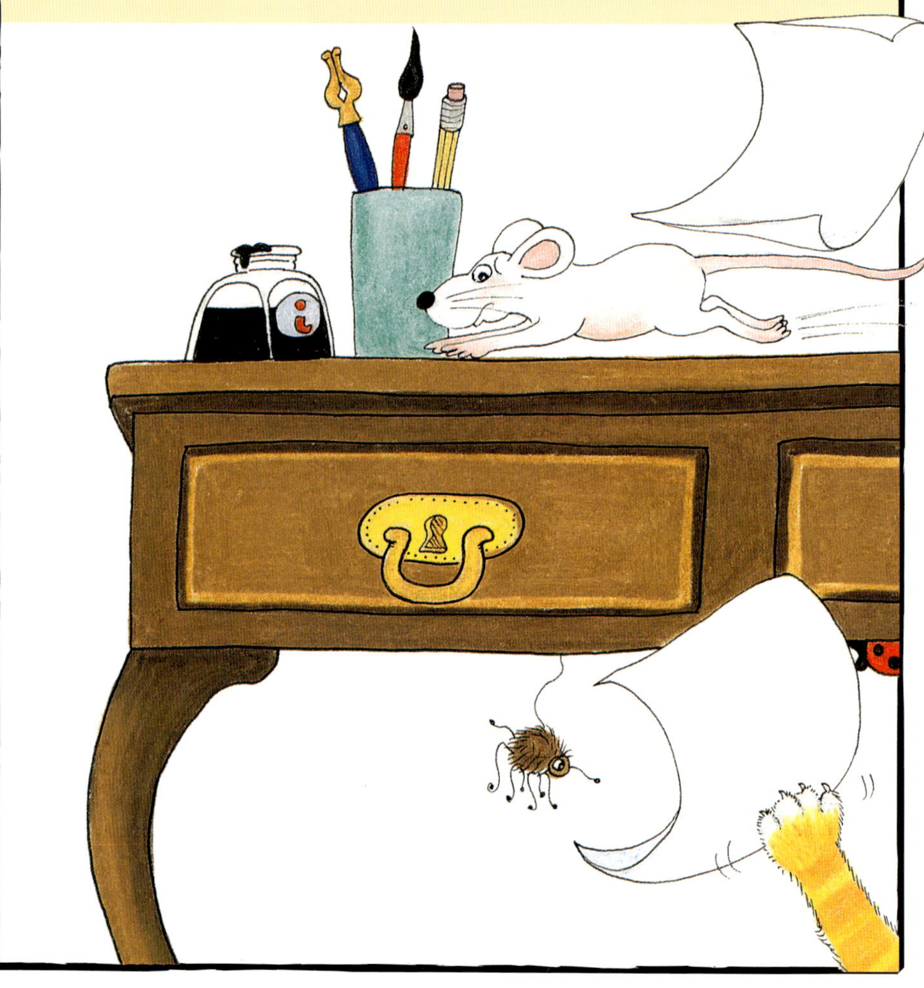

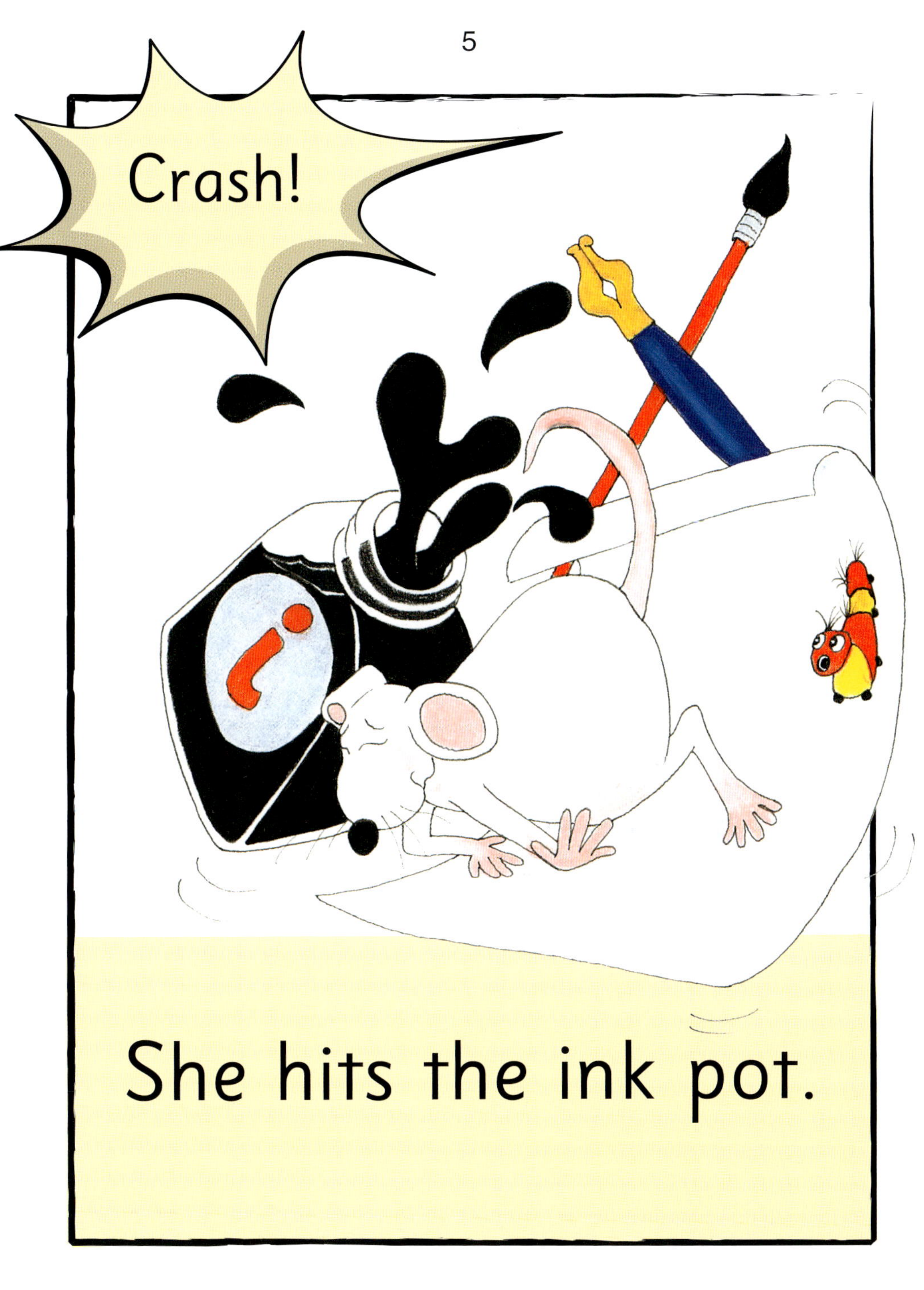

She hits the ink pot.

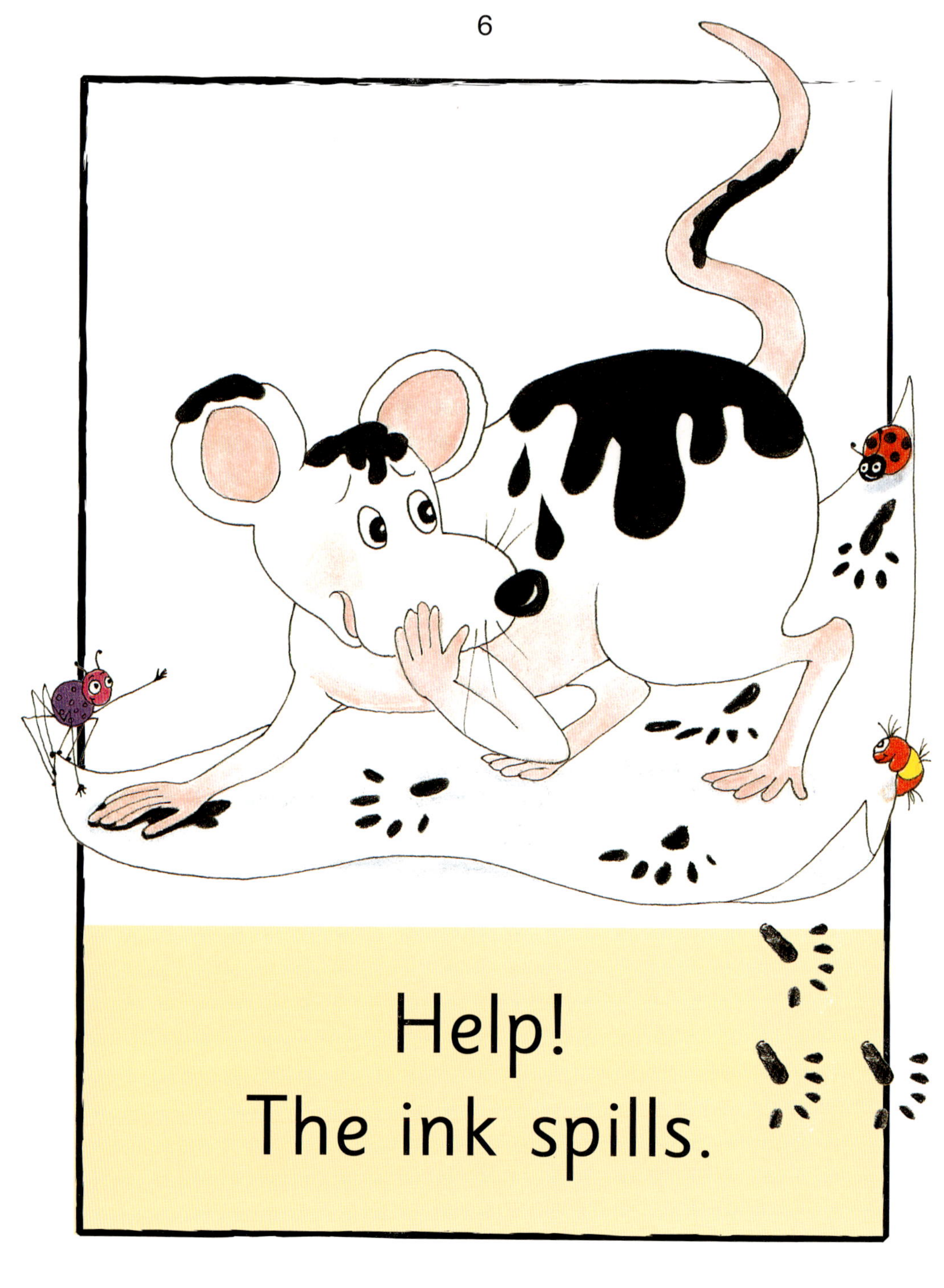

Help!
The ink spills.

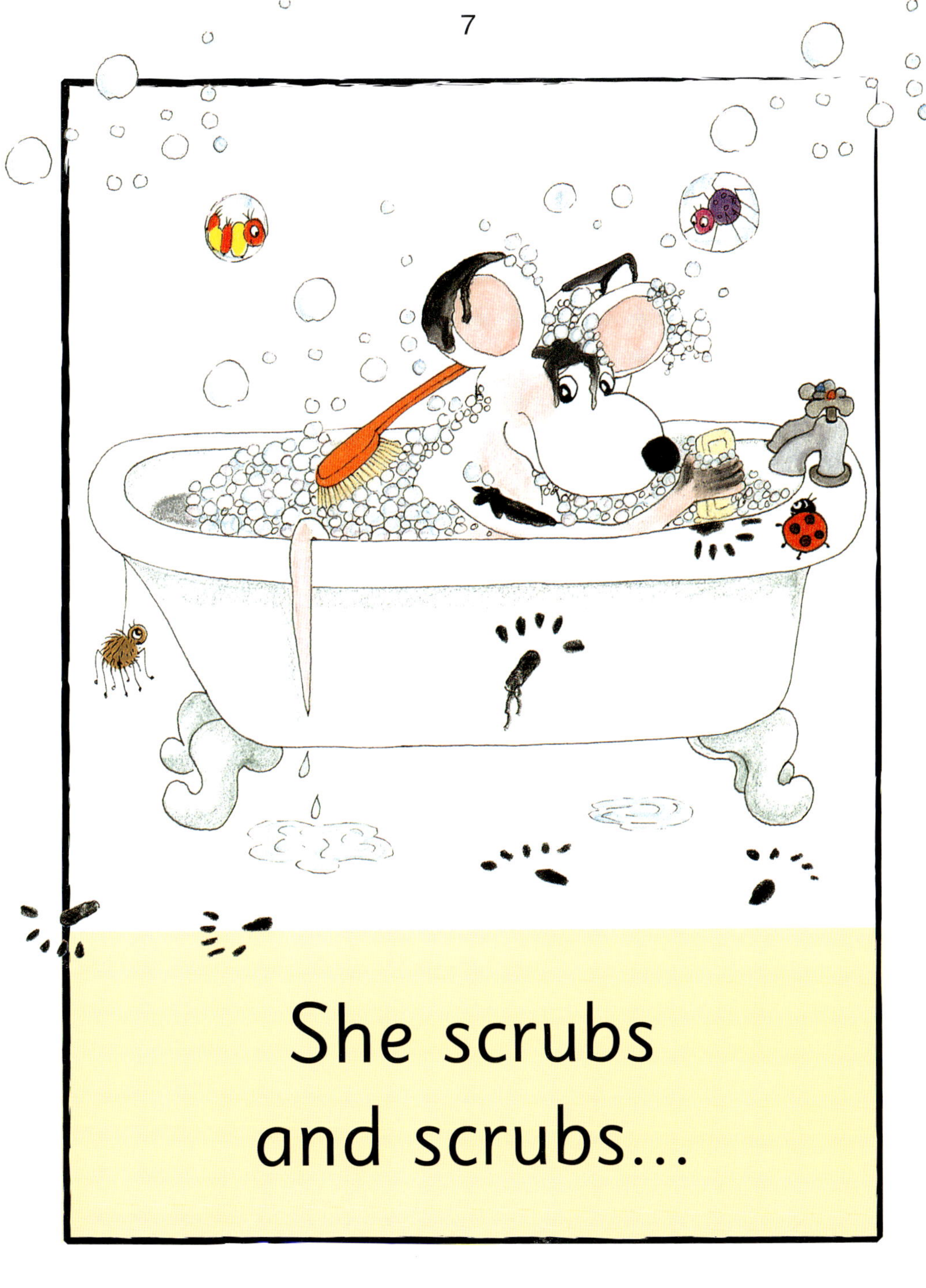

She scrubs
and scrubs...

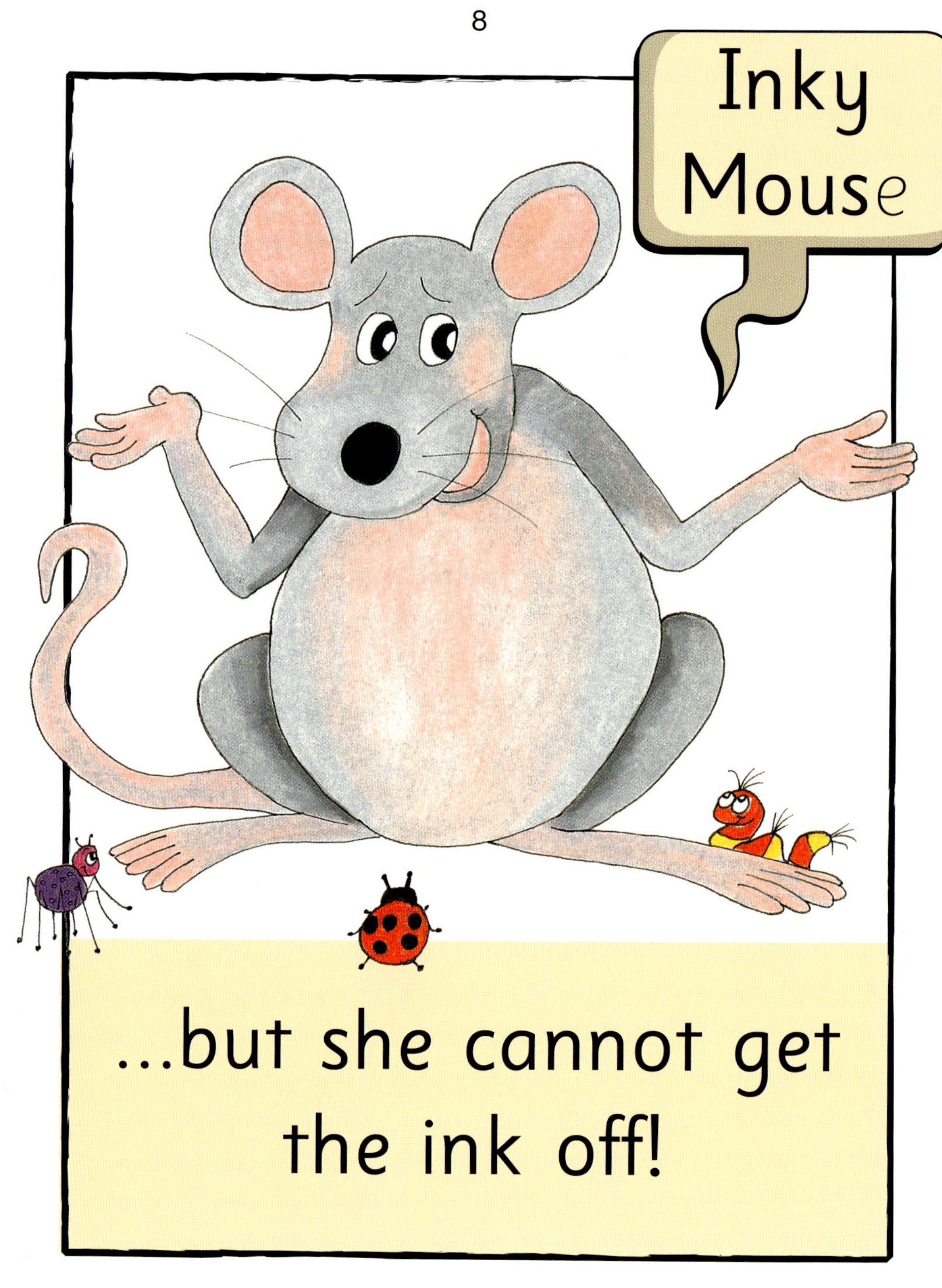

...but she cannot get the ink off!